LITTLE MISS SCARY

Roger Hargreaves

D0412765

Written and illustrated by
Adam Hargreaves

Little Miss Scary lived near the top of a mountain in a house called Spooky Cottage.

When it was dark she would creep into the valley below, making sure that nobody saw her . . .

3 Sixteen Beautiful Fridge Magnets – any 2 for £2.00!
inc.P&P

They're very special collector's items!
Simply tick your first and second* choices from the list below
of any 2 characters!

1st Choice
- [ ] Mr. Happy
- [ ] Mr. Lazy
- [ ] Mr. Topsy-Turvy
- [ ] Mr. Bounce
- [ ] Mr. Bump
- [ ] Mr. Small
- [ ] Mr. Snow
- [ ] Mr. Wrong
- [ ] Mr. Daydream
- [ ] Mr. Tickle
- [ ] Mr. Greedy
- [ ] Mr. Funny
- [ ] Little Miss Giggles
- [ ] Little Miss Splendid
- [ ] Little Miss Naughty
- [ ] Little Miss Sunshine

2nd Choice
- [ ] Mr. Happy
- [ ] Mr. Lazy
- [ ] Mr. Topsy-Turvy
- [ ] Mr. Bounce
- [ ] Mr. Bump
- [ ] Mr. Small
- [ ] Mr. Snow
- [ ] Mr. Wrong
- [ ] Mr. Daydream
- [ ] Mr. Tickle
- [ ] Mr. Greedy
- [ ] Mr. Funny
- [ ] Little Miss Giggles
- [ ] Little Miss Splendid
- [ ] Little Miss Naughty
- [ ] Little Miss Sunshine

*Only in case your first choice is out of stock.

--- TO BE COMPLETED BY AN ADULT ---

To apply for any of these great offers, ask an adult to complete the coupon below and send it with the appropriate payment and tokens, if needed, to MR. MEN OFFERS, PO BOX 7, MANCHESTER M19 2HD

- [ ] Please send _____ Mr. Men Library case(s) and/or _____ Little Miss Library case(s) at £5.99 each inc P&P
- [ ] Please send a poster and door hanger as selected overleaf. I enclose six tokens plus a 50p coin for P&P
- [ ] Please send me _____ pair(s) of Mr. Men/Little Miss fridge magnets, as selected above at £2.00 inc P&P

Fan's Name _____

Address _____

_____ **Postcode** _____

Date of Birth _____

Name of Parent/Guardian _____

Total amount enclosed £ _____

- [ ] **I enclose a cheque/postal order payable to Egmont Books Limited**
- [ ] **Please charge my MasterCard/Visa/Amex/Switch or Delta account** (delete as appropriate)

Card Number

Expiry date ___/___   **Signature** _____

MR.MEN   LITTLE MISS
Mr. Men and Little Miss™ & ©Mrs. Roger Hargreaves

CUT ALONG DOTTED LINE AND RETURN THIS WHOLE PAGE

3 Great Offers for MR. MEN Fans!

MR. MEN TOKEN

1 New Mr. Men or Little Miss Library Bus Presentation Cases

A brand new stronger, roomier school bus library box, with sturdy carrying handle and stay-closed fasteners.
The full colour, wipe-clean boxes make a great home for your full collection.
They're just £5.99 inc P&P and free bookmark!

☐ MR. MEN ☐ LITTLE MISS (please tick and order overleaf)

2 Door Hangers and Posters

In every Mr. Men and Little Miss book like this one, you will find a special token. Collect 6 tokens and we will send you a brilliant Mr. Men or Little Miss poster and a Mr. Men or Little Miss double sided full colour bedroom door hanger of your choice. Simply tick your choice in the list and tape a 50p coin for your two items to this page.

PLEASE STICK YOUR 50P COIN HERE

Door Hangers (please tick)
☐ Mr. Nosey & Mr. Muddle
☐ Mr. Slow & Mr. Busy
☐ Mr. Messy & Mr. Quiet
☐ Mr. Perfect & Mr. Forgetful
☐ Little Miss Fun & Little Miss Late
☐ Little Miss Helpful & Little Miss Tidy
☐ Little Miss Busy & Little Miss Brainy
☐ Little Miss Star & Little Miss Fun

Posters (please tick)
☐ MR. MEN
☐ LITTLE MISS

Mr Noisy chuckled again and walked back to
Mr Jelly's house. To have a look under Mr Jelly's bed!

"BOO!"

Just as it was getting dark, they hid behind a bush beside the lane that led up to Mr Jelly's house.

They waited until they saw Little Miss Scary's shadowy figure creeping past them.

Mr Noisy found Mr Jelly hiding under his bed, his teeth chattering in fear.

"Whatever's the . . . " began Mr Noisy, and then remembered himself. "Whatever's the matter, Mr Jelly?"

"It's . . . it's . . . L-L-Little Miss S-S-Scary," chattered Mr Jelly, trembling in fear. "Sh-sh-she keeps jumping out and shouting 'b-b-b-boo' at me."

Mr Noisy made Mr Jelly a cup of tea, calmed him down and told him what they were going to do.

Spookily, the door swung open by itself.

"Hello," called Mr Noisy as softly as he could, which for you or I would have been a shout.

Then he heard a chattering noise coming from the bedroom.

About a week ago, Mr Noisy went to see his friend Mr Jelly.

Mr Noisy was worried because he hadn't heard from his friend for ages.

When he got to Mr Jelly's house, he knocked on the door.

She even scared them right out of their socks.

"BOO!"

She scared them out of their wits.

"BOO!"

She scared them stiff.

"BOO!"

And do you know why Little Miss Scary did this?

For fun.

You see, she loved to scare people more than anything else in the world.

And she was very good at it.

"BOO!"

And when that somebody did, she would tiptoe up behind them, open her mouth wide and shout . . .

And there she would wait very quietly until
somebody came along . . .